FOUR YEARS AND TODAY

AN M/ENBY ROMANTIC COMEDY

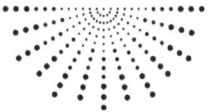

JAMIE SANDS

FOUR YEARS AND TODAY

BRIAR WOKE up from another dream about Nolan, and swore.

It had been yet another hot dream about Nolan taking them to bed, kissing them like they were precious, swearing his undying love.

They shouldn't be feeling like this about their best friend, there should be boundaries. Even if he was also their fake boyfriend.

The problem was, the fake boyfriend thing had been going on for years. If it had just been a few months, perhaps Briar wouldn't have fallen in love like this.

But no, it was literal years.

Four long, insufferable and undeniably wonderful years of pretending to be devoted to each other in public.

Briar was desperately, sickeningly in love, for real.

And they were sick of it.

Well, that wasn't exactly true. Briar wasn't sick of Nolan, or of spending time with him, or of having everyone look at them and say what a cute couple they made. Of feeling like they were a cute couple.

Briar was sick of pretending that all the huge wealth of affection they felt for Nolan was fake.

That Saturday morning they had woken up and decided to do something about it. Enough was enough. They couldn't keep suffering in silence. Leaning into the hugs and kisses and compliments that Nolan was probably doing for show and pretending they were real gifts for Briar.

So, mind made up, Briar showered and got dressed. What to wear was a conundrum. They wanted to wear something that Nolan had said he liked on them. But that didn't *really* narrow things down. They weren't feeling particularly masculine or feminine that day, so that didn't help with choosing either.

Finally, they settled on a pair of comfy but presentable baggy jeans and a buttoned shirt patterned with butterflies of all colors of the rainbow. They added one large dangling earring in one ear and several silver hoops in the other, styled their hair into a puffy quiff and put on the charm bracelet Nolan had given them on their last birthday.

They headed out of the apartment, bought a big bouquet of flowers (bluebells and carnations which were Nolan's favorites). They had to wait a few minutes for the train, but finally they got on the subway to tell him that they loved him for real, not just pretend. Their chest was full of tension, tightness, and their stomach was a nest for butterflies, but they didn't hesitate. This was the right thing to do.

* * *

Briar sat down in a free seat and took a deep, steadying breath. An elderly white lady in a floral dress smiled at them and the bright flowers. Briar smiled back, settled the flowers on their lap and let themself daydream. Not any old daydream though. They *remembered.*

It had started with a favor, that was all it was ever supposed to be. Nolan was going to a wedding for his cousin and his mother had insisted that he bring a date. Nolan was nursing the wounds from a particularly nasty break-up. Because of that, he'd come moaning to Briar.

Briar could remember it clearly, it was a Sunday, around eleven in the morning, and they'd only just finished making a huge batch of vanilla cupcakes. They were elbow deep in dishwater when he'd let himself in with the spare key.

He hadn't even offered to help with the dishes, he'd started whining right off the bat.

"She says 'find someone nice, and bring them along. You can't be the only one of your cousins who's single, I'll never hear the end of it.' Like it's that easy to go out, land a hot girlfriend or boyfriend, bring them to a wedding and act all nice and happy." He leaned back against the counter and dipped his finger in the frosting bowl.

"Maybe it is that easy," Briar had said. "Why don't I go with you? And don't eat the frosting with your fingers, you're not a four-year-old."

"Mean. I can't take you, Mom knows you." Briar found a clean teaspoon and offered it to Nolan so he could keep eating the leftover frosting. Indulging him, even then.

"Yeah, that's better if you think about it," Briar said. "No annoying interrogations over how you met them, what they do for a living, yada yada. She already knows, you can skip all that boring stuff."

"Hmmm. Mom does keep asking after you. She'd like to see you. But you'd have to really commit to it. I'm talking the whole hog. Dress up, co-sign the card, hang on my arm and everything. Act like you're in love with me."

"If it means you stop whining then I'm all in, when's the wedding?" They'd turned to Nolan and seen a softening of his features as he looked them up and down, something affectionate there. They'd flicked sudsy water at him to hide the warmth in their cheeks. "Focus. Answer my question."

"Saturday, two weeks time."

And so they'd gone to the wedding together. Briar had been on a masculine day, so dressed in a cream linen shirt, a fitted gray waistcoat and suit pants, a purple bow tie and a discrete enamel non-binary pride pin. Nolan had gone full suit with a pale blue tie and Briar had been secretly impressed by how handsome he scrubbed up. They had a pleasant time, seated with Nolan's cousins. They had an easy conversation over dinner, laughing and getting to know each other. Absolutely no one was weird about Briar's gender, which was an unexpected bonus. As the night wore on they drank champagne and ate wedding cake. Nolan even invited Briar to dance.

Briar leaned their forehead on the subway window and smiled, remembering Nolan's expression when he saw just how much Briar loved to dance at weddings. Briar danced with their whole body, their whole soul. None of that boring side to side swaying or awkward-uncle dancing. No, they threw themself into the song and took their partner along with them. It was excellent fun and always livened up the dance floor. Inspired others to do the same, to let loose and really make it a party.

They looked out, seeing mostly their reflection. Briar had thought the wedding would be the end of it, but then Nolan's Irish grandfather had passed away and they desperately wanted to support him through the funeral and wake. It had seemed uncouth to correct his grieving family about their relationship, definitely the wrong time. Besides that, Nolan had been sad and clingy. He was in need of human touch, so Briar was happy to provide that for him.

It had been easy to play along as the partner and make sure he ate and drank water, and got enough sleep while they were staying in a motel over the days of the funeral and wake.

* * *

Briar's phone buzzed and they pulled it out. Their phone lock screen was a selfie of themself with Nolan. His eyes were crinkled shut as he laughed, Briar kissing his cheek - a joke shot.

Just a joke, right?

Except that every time Briar sneaked a kiss with Nolan their heart fluttered with hope. Tingles also were often involved. Tingles that promise something more if only Nolan actually meant it.

Nolan had sent a message. Briar thumbed the notification but it was only a meme he'd found, nothing that needed a reply. They laugh-reacted it, and pocketed their phone again.

So, after the funeral, it had been about a month after that... they'd had The Conversation.

"My family is really happy we're together," Nolan had said. He'd rubbed his hand through the hair on the back of his neck, a move that made Briar perk up. It made him look so handsome, and it showed off his biceps. "I know it's a lot to ask, and it's kind of weird, but can we keep up the pretence?"

Briar had agreed embarrassingly fast. "Yeah, no problem here. I mean, it's not like I'm over here beating men off with a stick or anything."

Nolan smirked, his eyebrows raising "Is that what you're into? Beating men with sticks?"

"Only if they ask very very nicely," Briar said, loftily. Nolan had thwacked them with a cushion. He was over at their place again, it was just where they seemed to always hang out these days. Watching TV, playing video games, and so on.

"But actually, if you're okay with it," Briar's tone was meant to be casual but it sounded anything but to their own ears. "I'm heading to Vermont to have Christmas with my folks at the end of the year and it'd be brilliant if I had someone to protect me from the aunts. The aunts are always asking when I'm settling down, having babies, that kind of thing."

Nolan settled back on the couch and considered it. "Can we go skiing?"

"Sure, if you want?"

"Then I'm in. But, before we get there we should probably sort out if we're having kids or not." His eyes widened and he held up his hands. "I mean pretend us. Is pretend us planning on kids?"

Briar bit their lip, thinking. "I think so, one day. But not like, any time soon. I'm still wrapped up in getting everything sorted to open my own bakery, and then I'll be working hard on making it a success."

Nolan leaned over and ruffled their short hair, it had been dyed pink at that time. "Sounds good to me, fake enby-friend."

"Partner is a fine word," Briar said. "Let's stick with that."

Christmas in Vermont had been so easy with Nolan beside them.

They'd made cookies together, gotten each other gifts, made snowmen and non-binary snow people out the front of the house, and even gone to the local Christmas market arm in arm, looking at the lights and buying freshly roasted chestnuts and hot chocolate.

The aunts had loved Nolan, and spent all their attention on flattering him, knitting him sweaters and getting him to lift heavy things.

It had been a real joy, and so the next year he'd come along again, and the year after that.

"Doesn't your family want to spend Christmas with you?" Briar had asked, in the second year, as they booked flights for them both. Nolan shook his head.

"We do New Years, that's the big event. You should come, they missed you last year."

Briar had smiled, feeling warm and excited in a way they hadn't really before when they'd thought of New Years Eve. "Sure."

After that second Christmas with Briar's family and New Years with Nolan's family, they stopped holding back. It was accepted that if there was any event that one of them was doing, the other would come. An unspoken agreement that took the pressure off both of them. Their mutual friends, who had known about the 'fake dates' teased them relentlessly about how much they were actually smitten with each other. Nolan always rolled his eyes and denied it, so Briar did too, although it had started to hurt their heart, just a little, every time they did.

Before they started fake dating, when they were only friends (technically they were still only friends, but Briar didn't want that to be true any more), Nolan had been the first person Briar came out to.

They'd been in a food court when Briar did it. Briar eating yakisoba with fried tofu and Nolan eating mee goreng with chicken.

Briar had been trying to work up to it for days, maybe even weeks, and kept on chickening out. Non-binary wasn't that well known as an identity, there were still a lot of people who'd simply never heard of it, or who had the wrong idea about what it meant. Briar wanted Nolan to know their true self though.

So, after swallowing a piece of tofu and noodles, they cleared their throat. "Nolan, I'm trans."

Nolan looked up at them with wide eyes. "Okay?"

"Yeah, so I'm trans non-binary. I think genderfluid is the best word to describe what I am, but I'm still kind of working that out."

Nolan set his bamboo fork down and reached for Briar's hand. "Okay. What pronouns should I use for you, then?"

Briar let their hand be held as their eyes welled with tears and a lump spiked their throat.

7

"That's it? That's your whole reaction?"

Nolan squeezed their hand. "Yeah? Did you expect me to freak out?"

"Not exactly," Briar said. "But I thought ..."

"It honestly doesn't surprise me. You've been experimenting with different looks for more than a year now, B. I love you, you're my best friend, I'm here for you no matter what."

It was all the perfect words, the best possible response to them coming out. They couldn't help but cry. Free hand fumbling for their napkin they tried to swallow the tears. Crying in a food court, it was so embarrassing, but they couldn't help themself either.

Nolan squeezed their hand. "I want you to know you can be whoever you are with me, I won't freak out. I accept you, and I love you."

"Oh my god, please stop talking." Briar yanked their hand away from his to mop their face with the scratchy napkin. "Okay, good, you're perfect, thanks."

Through all the family get-togethers and work events, Nolan had been very consistent on introducing Briar with their pronouns. Making sure that if Briar was ever misgendered, they were swiftly corrected. It had been wonderful, having someone to clarify things so that Briar didn't have to explain themself every time.

Another reason to love Nolan, right there. He was the best ally, and partner, they could have possibly had.

Briar allowed themself the indulgence of thinking back to the first night they'd met Nolan.

Their mutual friend Bekka had introduced them at her birthday outing. They'd gone bowling and Briar had arrived late to find themself on the team with Nolan.

It was years ago now, thinking back Briar reflected how young they'd been.

Nolan, fresh-faced and sporting an actual vintage bowling

club shirt, had grinned at Briar and offered them some of his cheese nachos.

"You have a real bowling shirt." Briar said, through a mouthful of melted cheese sauce.

"I do, I found it in a thrift shop this afternoon." Nolan pointed proudly to the embroidered patch on his chest. "So for tonight my name is Frank."

Briar giggled. "I'm impressed you didn't say 'let me be Frank with you'."

"Oh trust me we heard that a lot when he first showed up." Bekka laughed affectionately and rolled her eyes.

"Good sense of humor." Nolan nodded approvingly at Briar.

"Did we just become best friends?" Briar had quipped, but been surprised to realize they hoped it was actually true.

Nolan nodded and handed them a bright green bowling ball. "Absolutely. Now, whoever loses this game buys drinks for everyone else."

"Bring it on." Briar hoisted the bowling ball and took their mark at the top of the alley, bowling a perfect strike on their first try.

They grinned, looking back at Nolan.

He was tugging on the sleeve of the bowling shirt and pretending to grimace. "I think I'm about to be hustled. I take it you've bowled before?"

"It used to be the thing my grandparents took me out to do every weekend." Briar ostentatiously inspected their nails. "Hope you weren't expecting an easy win."

"Nah." Nolan picked a purple ball from the return and swaggered up to the alley. "A challenge is always more fun."

* * *

Three years after their fake-dating arrangement began, Briar opened their own bakery. After a tough first six months barely

9

scraping by, it had gained popularity. There were often lines out the front before they opened, people competing to get the fresh cinnamon donuts that always sold out first. Nolan's work had also been successful, he'd started as a lowly intern, and now was a database architect at a large company, often on call in case of emergencies, which he didn't enjoy except for the bonus pay.

Briar opened their phone again and flicked back through the dates on their calendar - last year, the year they'd traveled for a *Fall's Dark Synergy* concert. Briar's favorite band and Nolan's third favorite. Mostly pop-punk, but with just enough gothic-country influence to be interesting. They drove upstate, booking a couple of nights at a bed and breakfast.

"I'm in my thirties," Nolan had said. "I can't drive three hours home after a freaking rock concert, I need to sleep."

"Agreed," Briar had said. "Old man."

"I am literally three months older than you."

"Yes." Briar had gently punched his shoulder. "You're an old man."

When they'd arrived, the day before the concert, the B&B had set them up in a room with only one bed. On the times they'd visited Briar's parents they'd avoided the 'only one bed' scenario easily. They slept in Briar's old room which had a trundle bed for Nolan.

But this room wasn't big enough to have a trundle bed. There was a big bed with a solid wooden bed frame, one small armchair, a grand old desk with a stack of magazines on it and then the bathroom.

"There's only one bed," Nolan said, as he closed the door.

"Yeah. One bed." Briar tried and failed to forget all the romantic stories they'd read where being forced into a single bed brought the couple closer to each other. Where stolen kisses and accidental cuddles led to more than either of them had ever expected. They tried their hardest not to want that.

For a moment neither of them said anything at all. Briar

cleared their throat, about to say they could go back to the reception and ask for a different room.

Nolan strode past them and set his bag down on the end of the bed.

"I sleep on the left side, hope that's not a problem for you, because I won't change it. So, if you have a problem with that, suck it up."

Briar cracked up. "I always sleep on the right, so you've lucked out on this one." They set their bag down beside Nolan's. "Keep your hands to yourself, all right?"

"Same goes for you." Nolan waggled a finger at them and then lowered it. "Except fair warning, I do get cuddly in the morning, like, before I really wake up."

The first night, Briar had woken in the small hours because Nolan had snuggled up to their back and slipped an arm around them. They had relaxed into his warmth and gone right back to sleep. In the morning, he'd rolled away as Briar was waking, and they couldn't bring themself to talk about it. To ask if it meant anything or it was just the sleepy cuddly thing he'd warned them about. Surely it was nothing. He was simply attracted to a warm body, if there'd been a teddy bear there he'd probably have cuddled it instead of them.

* * *

The *Fall's Dark Synergy* concert was that night. They stood towards the back of the crowd where there was decent distance between people and there was no danger of a mosh pit.

"I'm too short to get right in at the front," Briar said. "I don't want to get crushed or have someone spill their beer on me."

"Fine with me," Nolan said. "I've got a good view of the stage and the screens from here, I'm happy if you are."

Briar had looked at him and said rather too sincerely. "I'm

happy." Thankfully it was largely drowned out by a roar as the opening act took the stage.

The concert was wonderful, great openers, and *Fall's Dark Synergy* when they took the stage, was in brilliant form. They were full of energy and played a lot of Briar's favorite songs. Even still, they kept finding their attention drifting to Nolan. He was dressed in a *Fall's Dark Synergy* T-shirt he'd bought from the merch store, and he raised his hands in the air as he sang along, deep into the music.

Briar's chest tightened as they watched him. His slim hips swaying with surprising grace, his new shirt riding up to allow a glimpse of skin. He must have got a slightly-too-small size because it clung to his biceps as well. Had he been working out more? Briar couldn't remember his biceps being that large.

Sharing a bed that night had been considerably more difficult. Briar got into the bed and lay on their side, facing away from him. But Nolan's body heat made him impossible to ignore. Every time he moved or sighed or rearranged the pillows, Briar closed their eyes tight and tried to think pure thoughts.

The train shuddered, taking a corner a little too fast, jostling Briar out of their reverie. They checked the flowers were holding up alright, and took a look around the carriage. The little old lady had got off at some point, and where she had been sitting there were now three gothic looking teenagers, passing headphones between them. Briar wondered if there was any chance they listened to *Fall's Dark Synergy*? Probably not. That band had probably been around since before those teenagers were born.

Briar's window showed nothing but their reflection now, as the train thundered through a tunnel. They looked into their own eyes and *hoped*. They were reasonably certain that Nolan well... he may or may not return the depth of their feelings, but they knew at least that he liked them. He wouldn't have been so sweet at their last birthday if he didn't like them for real.

It had been a hard birthday in a lot of ways, falling as it did during one of the toughest weeks of the bakery's opening months. Briar had been seriously panicking over the costs of flour and sugar when most of what they were baking wasn't selling. They comforted themself on donating unsold goods to the local soup kitchen, but it had seemed dire. They were considering closing up shop.

On the day of their birthday, they headed home, feeling worn out and despairing at the fate of their little bakery. When they opened the door to their apartment, they were met with a loud roar "SURPRISE!"

Nolan had invited all their friends over, decorated the apartment with peonies and sunflowers (Briar's favorites) and they were all wearing silly headbands and hats. Briar was enveloped in the noise, and then in the arms of their friends as everyone wanted a turn to hug them. Finally they got to Nolan and he hugged them the tightest.

"Happy birthday," he said.

"I guess you used the key I entrusted you with to plan this?" Briar said, squeezing him.

"Oops, yes I did. Are you angry?"

"That was a total and complete betrayal of trust and I love it." Briar went up on their toes to kiss his cheek and he turned his mouth to reply at exactly the same moment. The accidental kiss sent intense tingles through Briar, and they quickly stepped back. Nolan's eyes had been sparkling, they were sure they hadn't imagined that.

Had he done it on purpose? Perhaps they could lean in for another kiss?

A champagne bottle popped, startling Briar back from Nolan, and then another friend appeared beside them with a sheet cake from Costco with their name spelled out in M&Ms on it.

"We know this isn't as delicious as your creations, but we didn't want to spoil the surprise and have you bake your own birthday cake." Nolan said.

"Any cake I didn't have to make is delicious." Briar grinned, as their friends began to sing happy birthday to them. The rest of the night was a whirl of sugar, champagne and laughter. Nolan was close by all night, but never within kissing distance, and Briar tried to let it go. It had just been a moment, a silly accident, and they shouldn't read into it, they knew that. The night had been wonderful, lifting their failing spirits immeasurably. He'd also given them the charm bracelet that night. Sterling silver with three charms on it; a little cupcake to signify Briar's bakery, a sunflower for their favorite flower and a little anatomically correct heart.

"That's a little morbid isn't it?" Briar had teased, dangling the heart with its aorta sticking out in front of their eyes.

"Well, you're a *Fall's Dark Synergy* fan," Nolan had said. "A little round heart with an arrow through it wouldn't fit the vibe."

Briar couldn't argue with that. They also wondered why Nolan had insisted on adding a heart to the charms, and not say... a friendship token of some kind.

They were very grateful to Nolan for making the surprise happen.

But they'd never forgotten that particular kiss. It hadn't been staged, or for anyone's benefit. It was an accident, but it was Briar's.

Their cheeks were heating up. They shifted a little, in their seat. Fingers straying to toy with the heart charm now. What had he meant by including it? Love? Platonic love or something more? He'd said the round heart with the arrow through it, which was a pretty clear message. But the anatomical one was more confusing, harder to decipher. Much like Nolan himself.

The train had gotten busier, and at the next stop Briar stood up to allow a pregnant woman to sit down in their seat. Holding onto the handrail with one hand, and their bouquet with the other, they braced against the rocking of the train.

They were over halfway to Nolan's stop. They wondered if they should have planned what they were going to say, but that seemed like a bad idea. They wanted to speak from the heart, even if it came out poorly, rather than have a rehearsed script. Nolan wouldn't respond well to a rehearsed script.

Nolan liked spontaneity.

He liked to turn up out of the blue and suggest a trip to the beach, or to a movie Briar wouldn't have ever considered seeing at the arthouse cinema near his place. He liked adventure. He'd never yet convinced Briar to go camping with him but they had a sinking dread that it was only a matter of time. They could only say no to him for a limited time before giving in to his charm. He was persuasive, and Briar was weak.

They remember the time he'd convinced them to attend a movie screening in costume. It was the twenty-fifth anniversary of *The Princess Bride*, a film they both had a lot of fondness for, and his weird arthouse cinema held a special event. Briar wasn't a huge fan of fancy dress and costumes, but Nolan had worn them down.

"Come on, it's not like *Rocky Horror* or something where people expect you to get up and dance," he'd said.

"I'm *never* going to *Rocky Horror*."

"I know. But this is *Princess Bride*! You love it. Briar, you can practically recite it."

Briar grumbled. Could already feel themself giving in, but resisted all the same. Nolan saying their name always made them weaker than it should.

"Imagine, we could take pictures together and get them made into Christmas cards and send them to everyone we know."

Briar fixed Nolan with a look. "That is not helping your cause in any way. I do not want fake couples Christmas cards."

"Okay, forget the cards. How about this, you dress up and come with me, and I'll pay for whatever you want from the concession stand."

Briar brightened, their resolve dissolving quicker than a sugar cube in hot tea. "You mean that?"

"Yes, just please say yes because I kind of maybe already bought the tickets and I literally have no one else to go with because the rest of our friends are boring and overworked..." He clasped his hands together and gave them his best puppy-dog look. He was so cute and so handsome and Briar knew that they'd agree with pretty much anything if it made him happy.

* * *

On the night of the film, they dressed up as Inigo Montoya, with drawn-on facial hair, and Nolan had made a very handsome Dread Pirate Roberts. They suspected that he'd hoped Briar would dress as Princess Buttercup, but they hadn't felt very feminine around that time.

Besides, the place, when they got there, was lousy with Buttercups. Nolan was asked for his photo every time they took two steps, and he'd gesture Briar in with him.

It took twenty minutes and dozens of photos to get into the cinema's lobby. Briar had a fine time indulging at the concession stand. Jumbo popcorn and soda, chocolates, candies, a hot dog, more than they could possibly hope to eat, but by that point it wasn't about actually eating it all. It was about seeing Nolan sweat. To Briar's disappointment, he took it all in his stride and even carried it all to their seats for them.

The audience was a warm one, laughing at all the jokes. True to his word there was no dancing, or getting up in front of everyone. Nolan and Briar had shared a massive bucket of popcorn and Briar had mixed M&Ms in once the corn had cooled enough to not melt them.

Briar had to admit it was a very fun night and one of their favorite memories. Their pockets full of uneaten snacks, they'd gone home and thought about how handsome a pirate Nolan had made while they showered.

Briar snapped themself out of it again. They couldn't afford to get *those* sorts of thoughts on the public train. They were on their way to tell Nolan that they loved him for real. They had to stay focused on that, on making it a good and positive experience. They could do that.

Their phone buzzed again and Briar checked it, another text from Nolan, asking what they were up to, how was the bakery?

Briar had taken to letting their second in command run the place on Saturdays, to give them time to work on accounts and paperwork, have a bit of a breather. Today that was all out the window. Nolan would think it was weird if they didn't reply to this message. They thumbed a quick reply 'all good, busy!' and pocketed their phone right in time for the train to brake - forcing them to grab onto the rail again.

They had so many lovely memories with Nolan, fun things, but they really valued the times he'd come through for them as a support. Eighteen months ago was the time Nolan had really pulled through and shown his true colors.

Briar's sister — elder by ten years — had called while Briar was in the dregs of the lunch rush one Thursday. Briar had picked up and heard her sister in tears.

"Astrid, what is is?"

Astrid swallowed audibly and stammered out the dreaded words. "I have a lump, they've just done a biopsy ... and... it's cancer."

"I'm on my way," Briar said. Their own eyes welled up.

"You don't need to," Astrid said, half-heartedly. "I'm not doing anything today, I have appointments later in the week—"

"No buts, I'm coming. You shouldn't be alone right now." Astrid lived alone after her polycule dissolved. Briar couldn't stand the thought of her sitting there alone with this news.

"I didn't say but." Astrid laughed wetly into the phone.

"Don't argue with me, I'm on my way."

Briar hung up the phone and a huge, wet sob erupted out of them. They startled the last remaining customers, who hurried out the door. Fair enough.

Briar swiped their eyes on their sleeve, scrawled '*closed for family reasons*' on a piece of paper, stuck it to the door and locked it.

Without really thinking about it, they called Nolan and set the call on speaker as they started packing the leftover baked goods into takeaway boxes. Thankfully it had been a relatively busy day and they wouldn't be overloaded.

"What's up?" Nolan's voice came through the tinny speakers and a sense of warmth and security flooded Briar's chest. "I have to head into a meeting."

"Astrid is sick, she's got—" Briar's voice faltered as their throat closed on a painful lump. They swallowed hard. "Um. She's got cancer."

"I'm so sorry, Bri. Are you okay? Is she?"

"No!" The tears were leaking out of Briar's eyes now. "I'm heading to her place, closed up early, and I'm going, so. I wanted you to know, I guess."

"I'll bring dinner. I have to go to this meeting but I'll come by later, okay?"

"You don't need to do that."

"I want to. Text me her address and I'll come by after work."

Briar's shoulders relaxed infinitesimally. "Thanks. Okay. Yeah." Briar hesitated, looked around and felt the panic rise again. "What was I doing?"

"Going to your sister's." Nolan prompted. "But, hold on, you're still in the bakery? Lock up the cash, put it in the safe.

Check the door is locked and that you didn't leave any windows open."

Briar blinked. They hadn't considered the cash. "Yes. good points."

Moving quickly around the shop floor, they checked the windows were closed and bolted, that the deadlock was on the door. Then they went to open the till, took the entire drawer out and shoved it into the safe with the day's receipts. They slammed it shut.

Nolan was still on the line. "That's all done."

"Grab your things. Jacket, key, wallet and go get a cab."

"It's all the way across town, I was going to get the subway." Briar's voice broke. The subway would take ages, and they wanted to be there *now*.

"I'll spot you the cash. No, better, I'll order a rideshare for you on my account. Text me the address and I'll sort it out, okay?"

Briar closed their eyes, eternally grateful for his level head and willingness to spend money. "You're too good."

"What else is a fake boyfriend for?"

The word fake actually hurt when he said it. A stab in the heart that Briar didn't, and couldn't deal with at that moment. They shook it off. "Texting you the address."

"Call me if you need to. I gotta go right now but I'll send you the rideshare details when it's on its way."

Thirty minutes later, Briar was hugging their crying sister. They couldn't have been there as fast on the train.

"Thanks for coming," Astrid had said. "The prognosis is actually pretty good but, ugh. It's so scary. As soon as the doctor said the word I just..."

"Whatever you need, I'm here for you." Briar promised.

By the time Nolan arrived it was past seven and Briar and their sister were sitting side by side on the couch watching soap operas and cackling at the actors. Briar got up to let him in and took a couple of the paper sacks from him.

"I wasn't sure what to get so I got deli sandwiches, nachos, burritos, some pasta and salad, doner kebabs, baklava and some cheese and crackers."

"You brought everything?" Briar laughed. "That's a lot of food."

"It's perfect. I love your baking Briar, but I'm sugared out." Astrid grinned as they carried the food in and started unpacking it on the coffee table. "This one's a keeper, Briar. I said it at Christmas, and I mean it even more now."

Briar agreed silently but shot an appreciative glance at Nolan, who was pouring drinks.

The evening ended up being very pleasant despite everything and a large part of that was Nolan's contribution, and his calm, steady presence.

Over the weeks and then months of treatments, Briar had been true to their word, going to appointments and treatments with Astrid, holding her hand, providing jokes, food, books of crosswords and a shoulder to cry on as needed.

In turn, Nolan was there for Briar, giving them space to decompress, making sure they ate as well, and picking them up when needed. He also assisted Briar in hiring their second in command to run the bakery when Briar couldn't be there, which had taken a huge load off their mind.

Astrid had responded well to treatment, and after a long ten months she'd been declared cancer free. All follow-up tests since then had come out clear.

Briar had coped with the stressful time as well as they had because of Nolan's support. They allowed themself an indulgent, private smile. Nolan had acted in every way as if he were a real boyfriend, not a fake one. Holding Briar while they cried, letting them crash out in his bed, providing coffee and granola in the morning. It hadn't felt fake at all, except for the times they'd wished they could kiss him and had to hold themself back.

* * *

The train rocked gently and Briar took a seat again. A large station, the last before Nolan's, had emptied out much of the carriage. It was nearly time.

They thought back, to the closest they'd ever come to the conversation they'd been about to have. It was two years into the fake dating experiment, two years ago now, and Briar had just accompanied Nolan to a work event. A social evening of drinks, nibbles and networking. They had enjoyed the evening, playing arm candy in a sparkling dress with a low V neck. They were in the elevator on the way out to grab something more substantial for dinner.

Briar had indulged in more than a few glasses of champagne, and it made them reckless. "Don't you ever want to..." they'd started to ask, and then been overcome with sudden shyness. Nolan's turning to them with a somewhat smoldering look as he loosened his work tie had absolutely nothing to do with it.

"Want to what?" he'd stepped closer, dropping his voice lower. If Briar hadn't known better they might have thought he was going to kiss them.

"Want to actually date someone?" Briar said. They were breathless, but they put it down to the champagne. "I mean, this arrangement we have is excellent and all, don't get me wrong, but isn't it sort of getting in the way of you finding true love?"

"Isn't it also getting in the way of *you* finding true love?" Nolan countered.

Briar's cheeks were too hot. Too much champagne. They were relieved when the elevator dinged, letting them out into the office lobby and then the chill air of the night. They pulled their shawl tighter around their shoulders.

"No, I'm not looking for anything." Briar shook their hair out and cleared their throat. "I'm focusing on my career, getting that off the ground right now. I don't have time for dates."

Nolan slipped his arm through theirs, casual as if they were actually on a date and hummed his agreement. "Same. My career is the most important thing right now, and if I get distracted at the moment I might miss out on an opportunity."

The relief washed over Briar like a warm shower. "Good, so we're in agreement, then."

"We keep up the pretense. Focus on our careers. If you want to actually date, like seriously, you have to let me know. I promise, there'll be no hard feelings."

"Yeah, no hard feelings." Briar had echoed. "Same for you." They said it, but they didn't mean it. If Nolan met someone and got in touch saying he wanted to date someone for real, Briar would ... well, they might go and hunt that person down and ensure it never happened.

But that was probably the champagne talking...even then they hadn't believed that as an excuse. They were nursing nascent feelings for their best friend, but it was fine. It didn't need to be dealt with. Things would go on as they were and it would be wonderful.

They'd had a pleasant evening at a late night diner and never talked about 'real' dates or 'true love' again.

That was changing today.

If Briar knew anything at all about true love they knew it meant Nolan.

Nolan was kind, funny, clever, affectionate, sexy and ... well, he was Nolan. He was everything Briar would want in a partner. There was no one who could ever compare. They just had to tell him that, and hope to the stars that he felt the same way. They were pretty sure he did. He'd never wanted to date anyone else after all, he was warm and affectionate with them, and he was always there if they called.

Sure, being there was a best friend thing too, but Briar was sure of the vibes. Sure enough to risk it all by putting their feelings out in the open and shooting their shot.

The train started to slow. Nolan's stop.

Butterflies hatched and flapped frantically around in Briar's stomach.

They clutched the bouquet and tried to steady their breathing. The train came to a stop and they got off the train.

It was a short walk up the block to Nolan's apartment building. A walk Briar had done hundreds of times, but it had never felt this frightening before. Briar felt like all eyes were on them, as if they were the lead in a movie and the cameras had zoomed in on their face, the lights all spotlighting their stride towards his building.

Flowers in hand like a sword, heart pounding as if they were about to slay a dragon.

But the building, when they got to it, was just a building.

A building so familiar.

They'd helped Nolan move in, after all. Only a few months ago. His old place had been dreadfully small, full of mold clusters and mice. Briar had been so relieved when he'd finally found a new place.

This building had a reliable elevator, central heating and plenty of room for all of Nolan's books. Thinking back to all those boxes of books, Briar's back still twinged with aches. Nolan read everything: fantasy, science fiction, horror, narrative nonfiction, anything he liked the look of. He was voracious, reading authors from all over the world, modern and classic. It was rare he couldn't find something to love in a book. He thrived on the different perspectives, diverse mythologies and seeing the world through someone else's eyes.

It was one of the main things Briar adored about him.

They'd gone to hire the moving van together and the rental guy had assumed they were married. The idea of it had filled Briar with indescribable joy. Butterflies upon butterflies in their stomach.

Nolan hadn't corrected the rental guy, but he'd laughed about it once they were in the car. The butterflies had calmed down, Briar laughing as well, brushing it off as best they were able. It wasn't their fault if a wedding ceremony had featured in several of their daydreams since that day.

Briar entered the lobby of Nolan's building and made their way to the elevator. The day they'd moved Nolan in had been long and arduous, but Briar hadn't minded at all. They'd imagined they were moving in together.

That was how pathetic they'd been.

Briar punched the button for Nolan's floor and hoped to whatever gods and powers in the universe were listening that Nolan felt the same way. That these years as best friends fake dating had changed the way he felt as well. Opened his eyes in some way.

The elevator dinged.

It was time. Taking a deep breath, Briar stepped out.

Condensation gathered on the cellphone that wrapped the flower stems from Briar's grip.

Their stomach turned over and they swallowed, throat parched.

What if this was all a mistake?

What if Nolan laughed in their face?

They'd ruin their friendship.

They'd lose their built-in date for whatever event they needed him for.

They'd lose their Nolan.

That was the thought they couldn't bear at all. They needed him. Life without Nolan would be so cold and gray.

Briar closed their eyes and thought of all those little

moments that had given them hope. The private smiles he'd given them. All the ways he'd gone above and beyond with things he'd done. They knew Nolan and with that knowledge came a small certainty that he wasn't faking his affection. He was faking the dates, the boyfriend status, but not the affection.

He took every opportunity to touch them didn't he? He checked in on them. He was there the second they were in need. It had to mean something.

Steeling themself, Briar knocked on the door to Nolan's apartment.

They had a key to his place, but this didn't seem like the occasion to let themself in.

They lowered their hand and were struck with a terrible new fear: What if Nolan had spent the night with someone?

Someone he'd picked up at a club or met on a dating app?

Nolan hadn't *said* he was planning on going clubbing and he'd never mentioned being on a dating app. But then, if he was, would he mention it to his fake partner? They could be about to interrupt something super awkward.

As Briar turned to chicken out and run away, the door opened.

They turned back.

Nolan smiled down at them, his eyebrows rising.

"Hey B, I didn't know you were dropping by."

He was dressed in a soft blue sleep shirt and green flannel pants. His pajamas. Briar's throat threatened to close up.

"Right. No, I didn't say anything, I just…"

Nolan opened the door to let them in. "Did you forget your key?"

"No, I have it." Briar gave himself a mental shake. "I made a decision and I wanted to follow through on it."

"Oh-kay." Nolan drew out the word, the way he did when he didn't believe them. "Cup of coffee? Tea?"

"In a moment." Briar walked inside and took a deep breath.

The smell of Nolan permeated this place, warm, familiar and beloved.

It was now or never.

But what were they going to say?

"Nolan, I'm...." the words died on their tongue. Why had they wanted to do this spontaneously? They should have planned what they were going to say! Now they were tongue-tied and blushing and Nolan was watching, perplexed as they fumbled.

Briar's mind was empty.

There was a long, agonizing silence.

Finally, Nolan broke it. "Who are those flowers for?"

That, at least, they could answer. They thrust the bouquet towards him, wincing as some petals floated to the ground. "You. I got them for you."

Nolan's confused expression switched to a warm smile. "Aw. You shouldn't have. It's all my favorites." He took the flowers from them and set them on his sideboard.

"Yeah. Because." Briar straightened their spine. They couldn't look directly at him and say this, so they closed their eyes. "I bought you flowers because I love you and I want us to date for real and not for fake and maybe we could get married someday and get cats and foster kids maybe? I don't know. I'm getting ahead of myself and I shouldn't do that, but I think you're the most wonderful person in the world and I love you."

"How about you come and sit down?"

Briar opened their eyes.

Nolan had moved closer. He gently but firmly took their elbow and guided them to his sofa. They'd even picked this out together. They'd sat and watched movies and played Mario Kart on it. Briar had fallen asleep on one occasion and woken up to a woolen blanket laid over them and their head in Nolan's lap. He had rested one hand on their shoulder, he'd been asleep too, his head thrown back.

It had to mean something, moments like that.

They sat down on the soft cushion and Nolan sat close by.

Briar clasped their hands and placed them between their knees. "Sorry. I know that was a lot."

"You could say that."

Briar couldn't read his tone. They chanced a glance at him. He looked concerned more than anything else.

"So... you're killing me here. Tell me what you think?"

"Are you breathing now? You looked so pale and you said all that stuff so quickly I thought you were going to pass out."

"I'm fine." Briar took a demonstrative breath. They looked at him significantly. "Please answer the question."

"Yeah."

Nolan said it off-handedly, like Briar had suggested they go see a movie. They had no idea what that 'yeah' meant. Their heart sped up. Did he mean Briar was being too much? Did he mean he loved them back? Did he mean yeah as in 'I need some time to process this'?

They squeezed their hands hard between their knees.

"Say. More."

"Right, okay, but you have to look at me."

Briar's mind went into overdrive. *Oh no, oh no this is where he lets me down easy and I'll probably pass out and then once I come to I'll never be able to look him in the eyes ever again.*

With a huge reluctance, Birar freed their hands from between their knees and half-turned, folding one leg under themself on the sofa so they could face Nolan.

To their absolute horror, he took both their hands in his and looked deep into their eyes.

"Yeah, I agree," he said. "We shouldn't fake date any more. I'm sick of pretending. Let's date."

His words took an embarrassingly long moment to process.

"Wait, what did you just say?"

"I agree we should date."

Briar searched his face, heart in their mouth, heart thundering. Could it be true?

"Say more?"

Nolan squeezed their hands, one thumb rubbing the back of their right hand.

"Briar, you're my best friend, but sometimes you're so obtuse it's hilarious. I'm in love with you, too. I have been since the beginning. I want to date you for real and getting married and maybe adopting foster kids and cats sounds wonderful to me."

Briar breathed out, their heart calming down. They dared to smile. "If you're messing with me, if this is a joke, I swear to the stars I'm going to have my righteous revenge on you."

Nolan tugged sharply on their hands at the same time he leaned in. He stopped their words, their worries and their doubt with a warm kiss.

They'd kissed before, but never like this. Cheek kisses, sure. Chaste pecks on the lips for the look of the thing. But this kiss was true. This kiss was passion and yearning and happiness.

Briar made a soft, high-pitched noise, unable to suppress their relief or their pure, unfettered *want*.

Nolan dropped their hands in favor of wrapping his arms around them. Briar surged forward, going to their knees to press themself against him, one arm curling around his waist, the other going to his hair to run their fingers through the soft strands.

Their fears evaporated into pure joy and excitement.

Nolan felt the same way!

Nolan loved them and had for some time. Nolan was theirs in a way he never had been truly before. Or possibly, he had always been, but Briar hadn't realized it.

There was nothing in their way now. He loved them, and he wanted to be with them and that meant they could kiss as much as they wanted to.

Nolan broke the kiss and they pulled back infinitesimally to look at him. His pupils were blown, his lips slightly parted and his hair mussed.

"Beautiful." Briar breathed the words, softly. "Nolan, you're so beautiful."

Nolan's cheeks pinked, more than they had been. Briar moved their hand from the downy hair at the back of his neck to brush his cheekbone with their thumb.

"I can't believe you feel the same way."

Nolan turned his head to kiss their palm and then looked into their eyes again.

"Believe it. You're my gorgeous, funny, clever and kind best friend. I love you, I'm so in love with you."

Briar closed their eyes and leaned their forehead on his shoulder. "I don't think I'll ever get tired of hearing that."

"You'll hear it a lot going forward."

They kissed again. This one lacked the same urgency but it was no less delightful. Briar's heart tugged and they gripped Nolan as tight as if they thought he might fly away.

They didn't want this moment to end. But nothing lasts forever, not even the best kisses in the world.

They pulled apart and Nolan nodded once. "Tea or coffee?"

"Tea please." Briar took a moment to fix their own hair, and get their breathing under control.

Nolan went into the kitchen to make tea and after a moment, Briar followed with the flowers, finding Nolan's only vase, filling it with water and putting the flowers inside.

They took them back out to the sitting room and placed them on the table. Nolan came out a few minutes later with cups of tea. They sat beside each other.

"So, what now?" Briar asked.

Nolan leaned against the back of the sofa and hummed a little. "Well, all our friends pretty much think we're already dating, and just saying it's fake, so they're probably wondering why we've taken so long to move in together."

Briar's heart skipped. "Yeah, probably."

"So, why don't you move in with me?"

Briar sucked on their lip and considered it. They wanted to live here. They'd imagined it after all. But it would mean a longer commute to their bakery. But... they could manage that if it meant being with Nolan every night and waking up to him every morning.

"Great, yes, when?"

Nolan chuckled. "As soon as you like."

Briar beamed. "I have nothing else planned for this weekend, so I could bring some things over this afternoon? If that's not too soon."

"I've been waiting four years, B. It's not too soon." Nolan squeezed Briar's knee. "Tea, then let's go get some lunch, head back to your place, pick up some bags and then come back here."

"I love that plan. I love you."

* * *

Three weeks later

Briar took the subway to Nolan's ... no, their place. The day had been long, a difficult day. One of their kitchen hands had called in sick, and they'd had to juggle baking with filling out tax forms. They felt bone-weary and ready to flop on the couch and do absolutely nothing.

They got off at their station and walked the short distance to the apartment building.

They thought of how nervous they'd been, on that Saturday, heading over to Nolan's with flowers brandished like a weapon and smiled.

They should have trusted their gut. Their gut had known

Nolan was fond of them, and it had been proved right. Their brain was to blame, second-guessing and doubting that there could be more. Nolan had been wonderful to live with and the transition from friends fake-dating to real-dating had been seamless.

In the mornings Briar got up obscenely early to get to the bakery, leaving Nolan snoozing in bed. When they got home, they had the apartment to themself for an hour or two, and then Nolan would get in from his job.

Together they'd make dinner, or order in, or eat out, and chat about their days. They'd touch, kiss, cuddle. Every kiss felt like a precious gift to Briar, even after it had happened more times than they could count.

They'd go to bed and explore each other anew. They were so hungry for each other, for people who knew each other so well, this was still unchartered territory. Briar loved every second of it. Finding out what they could do to make Nolan laugh, or moan, or shiver... They couldn't wait for that night, when they went to bed again. Briar was tired out from their day, but somehow Nolan always sparked new energy in them.

Their face flushed as they took the elevator and they tried to set aside the steamy thoughts for the moment. It was hard though, Nolan's bare chest flashed through their mind, and his round, squeezable ass, and the way his lips... *no*. Not right now.

Nolan ought to be home already, perhaps they could forget about dinner and just drag him straight to bed. They were sure he wouldn't mind such a disruption to whatever he was doing.

Briar unlocked the door and opened it, only to be immediately met with a roar of voices.

"SURPRISE!"

Briar's heart raced and their hand flew to their mouth.

Their friends were all in the apartment, which was decorated with white streamers and flowers on every flat surface.

A surprise party? But for what?

It wasn't their birthday.

"What?" Briar managed to breathe.

As if it had been rehearsed, the wall of friends parted in the middle, and there was Nolan. He was dressed in his nicest charcoal suit and the pink shirt Briar had helped him pick out.

He met Briar's eyes with a twinkle and sank to one knee.

Briar had been walking towards him on instinct. When he took up that position, they gasped and tears welled.

"Nolan, what?" They breathed.

Nolan produced a small velvet box, and licked his lips. He was nervous.

"Briar, you're the love of my life. I have been so happy these last few weeks, and before that, pretending to be with you. It's always felt like the most comfortable, most natural thing in the world to me. I love you. I want to make it permanent, for real."

Briar's tears dripped down their cheeks but their smile was so wide it hurt their cheeks. "Nolan..."

"Please, Briar, will you do me the honor of marrying me, and being my huswife?"

Briar nodded, covered their face with both hands and howled.

Around them their friends cheered and clapped, the sound drowning out Briar's sobs. Nolan was there a moment later, his arms around them, steadying them. They inhaled the scent of him and relaxed, dropping their hands and going on their toes to kiss him.

"I love you too, Nolan."

"So that's a yes?" Despite all the ruckus and the kiss, he was apparently still unsure.

"Of course it's a yes, you ridiculous boy." Briar pulled back. Taking a moment to mop up their tears with a tissue offered by their friend Bekka. Then they stuck out their hand. "Now give me that ring!"

There was a laugh from the crowd.

Nolan's eyes glinted as he slipped the ring onto their left hand. Briar threw their arms around him for a deep, delicious kiss. The kind of kiss that promised many more after it, that sealed their decision and tasted of the future.

They pulled apart after a moment and were instantly enveloped by their friends.

Briar hugged Bekka first. Then Astrid was in front of them. Someone in the back started playing music. *Fall's Dark Synergy*, of course. Briar recognized the live album they'd released of the concert they'd seen with Nolan.

"Astrid, you're here too?"

"Of course, Nolan called everyone! Mom and Dad couldn't make it, but they sent their love and said to call tomorrow."

Briar hugged their sister tightly and felt tears well again. Nolan was just too perfect.

Their cheeks hurt from smiling so much. Nolan took their hand and led them to the kitchen table. It was laden with food, but in the center was the *pîece de resistance*, a bright green cake roughly cut into the shape of a globe. The frosting was lumpy and there were three black blobs on it.

"I made you a cake."

Briar was too happy and giggly to hold back their laughter. "It's... what is it supposed to be? The Earth?"

"No, it's a bowling ball." Nolan slipped his arms around them from behind and rested his chin on their shoulder. "On the night we first met you used a green bowling ball."

Briar's laughter died, replaced with pure affection. "You remembered."

"Of course I remember."

"I love you." Briar turned just enough to kiss him softly on the lips. Then they turned back to the cake. "I appreciate the gesture, I do, but please, let me make the cake for our wedding, yeah?"

"That's probably for the best." Nolan laughed. "If I can be frank with you, I really had trouble with the frosting. It kept on separating and then it wouldn't stick to the cake itself, and it took hours."

"I love it. I love you. I love this." Something about what he'd said processed slowly. "Did you just make that frank joke because of your old bowling shirt?"

Nolan grinned, and pointed at the cake again. "I was wondering about doing a *Princess Bride* theme but this seemed easier somehow. Until I was doing it, anyway."

"We could do that for the wedding?" Briar leaned back against him and closed their eyes. "I can't believe we're going to get married."

"Believe it." Briar turned in Nolan's arms to kiss him once more. Around them their friends laughed and took photographs. Briar wanted to remember this moment forever, the culmination of over four years of pretending to love, while both of them, secretly were really in love. The future was so bright, so full of exciting promises, but they didn't ever want to lose track of the little moments. Because it was in the little moments that they'd realized their love for Nolan. They would hold these moments to their heart and hold them forever.

Nolan broke the kiss and the two of them turned, flushed and smiling to wave at their friends.

"Cut the cake!" Bekka shouted.

"I can't guarantee it's even edible," Nolan warned. He took the knife Astrid was holding out to him, and then passed it to Briar. "Come on, you're the expert, you cut it."

"And if the knife comes out clean you get a wish!" Bekka shouted. She looked like she'd had a few glasses of champagne.

Briar took the knife and carefully cut through the cake. When they withdrew the knife, it was clean of frosting, without a single crumb. They closed their eyes and wished with all their heart.

May today be the worst day of the rest of our lives. May we always keep growing, learning and loving each other. May we love each other more every day and grow old and happy together.

When they opened their eyes it was to see Nolan smiling at them, the sparkle in his eyes reflecting their wish.

SANTA'S SACKING

AN M/ENBY SWEET WITH HEAT CHRISTMAS ROMANCE

https://books2read.com/santasacking/

Darian knew from the moment Nole Ox took over BirdTalk that their ideal job writing code for a social media platform was done.

They packed up their things and went home to Snowfall, Oregon, tail between their legs for a quiet Christmas with their folks.

However, their folks want Darian to stay busy by contributing to the community so Darian finds themself signed up to help with the Christmas pageant. Thrown in at the deep end and with only days until Christmas, their only lifeline is handsome Connor, the handsome barista-turned-handyman.

Can Darian make the sound tech work so the kids have their musical cues?

Is Connor really the perfect hunk he appears to be?

And why can't Darian just sleep in?

Santa's Sacking is a sweet, tropey Christmas story that will fill your heart and tickle your funny bone. This story is Standalone but there *may* be a return to Snowfall for next Christmas...

THE FAIRYLAND SERIES BY JAXON KNIGHT / JAMIE SANDS

Book one: Rival Princes - a rivals to lovers romance with competing handsome princes

Book two: Mischief and Mayhem - the grumpy one, the sunshine one and a roller coaster

Book three: Recipe for Chaos - a billionaire romance, featuring instalove for the billionaire and a chef who isn't impressed with money

Book four: The Good, the Bad and the Dad - the start of a sweet menage with a single dad, a handsome prince and a mischievous pirate

Novella: Tailor Made Christmas - a second chance romance featuring a tailor and a prince, set after book four

Short story: New Year's Eve, the characters from Recipe for Chaos have a night to remember

Book five: The Trouble with Order - hurt and comfort opposites attract when Link gets a new villain

Buy now

There are three golden rules for new recruits at Fairyland
Theme Park:

1. No breaking character, even if you're dying of heat exhaustion
   2. Always give guests the most magical time
   3. No falling in love.

Nate's only been at work one day, and he's already broken all
three.

Fast-tracked into a Prince role, Nate's at odds with Dash, the
handsome not-so-charming prince who is supposed to be
training him. Nate doesn't know how he ended up on Dash's bad
side, but the broody prince sure is hot when he gets mad.

Dash has worked long and hard to play Prince Justice at
Fairyland. Now, instead of focusing on his own performance, he
is forced to train newbie Nate to be the perfect prince. Nate's
annoying ease with the guests coupled with his charm and good

looks could dethrone Dash from his number one spot ... so why does he secretly want to kiss him?

Fairyland heats up as sparks fly between the two rival princes. Will they get their fairytale romance before they're kicked out of Fairyland for good?

Find out in this standalone MM contemporary romance by Jaxon Knight, set in an amusement park where fairytales can come true.

ALSO PUBLISHED BY GREY KELPIE STUDIO

OVERDUES AND OCCULTISM BY JAMIE SANDS

A witch in the broom closet probably shouldn't be so interested in a ghost hunter, right?

That Basil is a librarian comes as no surprise to his Mt Eden community. That he's a witch? Yeah. That might raise more than a few eyebrows.

When Sebastian, a paranormal investigator filming a web series starts snooping around Basil's library, he stirs up more than just Basil's heart.

Between Basil's own self-doubt, a ghost who steals books and Sebastian, an enthusiastic extrovert bent on uncovering secrets, Basil's life is about to get a lot more complicated.

Overdues and Occultism is a sweet, no heat contemporary novella about a witch living in Auckland, New Zealand. MM romance, HEA.